THE MOSQUITO KING

AN AGATE AND BUCK ADVENTURE

BY SCOTT R. WELVAERT
ILLUSTRATED BY BRANN GARVEY

Librarian Reviewer
Marci Peschke

Reading Consultant
Elizabeth Stedem

www.raintreepublishers.co.uk
Visit our website to find out
more information about
Raintree books.

To order:
☎ Phone 0845 6044371
🖹 Fax +44 (0) 1865 312263
💻 Email myorders@capstonepub.co.uk

Customers from outside the UK please telephone +44 1865 312262

Raintree is an imprint of Capstone Global Library Limited, a company
incorporated in England and Wales having its registered office at 7 Pilgrim
Street, London, EC4V 6LB – Registered company number: 6695582

"Raintree" is a registered trademark of Pearson Education Limited,
under licence to Capstone Global Library Limited

Text © Stone Arch Books, 2008
First published in United Kingdom by Capstone Global Library in 2010
The moral rights of the proprietor have been asserted.

Edited in the UK by Laura Knowles
Art Director: Heather Kindseth
Graphic Designer: Kay Fraser

Photo Credits
Karon Dubke, cover (map)
Kay Fraser, cover (background images)
Originated by Capstone Global Library Ltd
Printed and bound in China by CTPS

ISBN 978 1 406215 89 2 (hardback)
14 13 12 11 10
10 9 8 7 6 5 4 3 2 1

ISBN 978 1 406216 09 7 (paperback)
14 13 12 11 10
10 9 8 7 6 5 4 3 2 1

British Library Cataloguing in Publication Data
Welvaert, Scott R.
The Mosquito King. -- (School mysteries)
813.6-dc22
A full catalogue record for this book is available from the British Library.

CONTENTS

Chapter 1

THE FEVER

Three figures on horseback headed down a trail under a hot sun. The vast Canadian wilderness stretched out beyond them. The man and two children had been travelling for days, through thick forests and over tall hills. They had almost lost track of what day it was.

The man riding in front was dressed in the bright red uniform of the Canadian Mounted Police. His name was Thomas Malloy. He turned in his saddle to look at the children, Agate and Buck McGregor, riding behind him.

"Just over the next rise, you two," said the Mountie, "we'll be able to see Adder Creek."

"Great," said Buck. The sixteen-year-old boy did not sound excited.

"I am sure that your aunt and uncle will be happy to see you," said the man.

"Yes, I know they will," said the girl.

"Agate," whispered Buck quietly to his eleven-year-old sister. "What's going on?" He pointed at the necklace Agate wore. It was giving off a soft blue light.

Agate grabbed the stone hanging from its cord around her neck. It felt warm.

"Someone needs our help," said Agate. She looked at the tall evergreens surrounding them. "I think it's someone close, Buck."

"But Uncle Alba is expecting us," said Buck.

His voice was louder than he meant it to be, and the Mountie turned. "Did you say something?" Thomas Malloy asked, smiling.

"No, sir," said Buck.

"How long will it take us to get to Adder Creek?" asked Agate.

The Mountie put his gloved hand up to shield his eyes and gazed up toward the sun. "I'd say about another hour," he said.

"That's too long," Agate whispered to her brother. The stone was almost burning her hand. "We are needed now!"

Agate and Buck pulled their horses' reins to slow them down. Buck hated to trick the Mountie – before their father died, he had been a Mountie, too. But Agate and Buck were needed elsewhere. Quietly, while the Mountie's horse headed over the next hill, Agate and Buck turned and raced off into the forest.

Miles away, in a town called Booker, a young girl lay on her bed. Her skin was covered with a bright red rash. She was soaked with sweat. Her mother knelt by her and wiped her face with a wet cloth.

The bedroom door burst open and a doctor rushed in. He set down his medical bag and rolled up his sleeves. Then he washed his hands in a basin of water on the dresser.

"How long has she had the fever?" the doctor asked.

"It's been three days now, Dr Copper," said the girl's mother. "I iced her down, but nothing seems to stop it."

Dr Copper wiped his hands with a towel and walked over to the girl. He laid his hand on her forehead. "She's burning up," he said.

The doctor opened his bag.

He took out a stethoscope and placed the drum on the girl's chest. But as he did, the girl sprang out of the bed and scratched the doctor across the face with her fingernails.

"No, Emily! No!" said her mother.

The doctor fell backwards in shock. Emily hid in the corner and hissed at them.

Dr Copper felt his face and then looked at the blood streaked on his hand.

The doctor moved closer to Emily. She turned away and started scratching at the wall.

A large, oozing, red sore was on the back of her neck.

"She said a mosquito bit her," said the girl's mother.

The doctor shook his head. "I've never seen a bite like that!"

– Chapter 2 –

BLACK CELLS

Agate and Buck rode all night long. Dawn was breaking when they arrived in the small town of Booker. Mist floated above their horses' hooves and the sky was full of clouds.

Agate held her glowing stone in front of her face. She turned to Buck and said, "We're getting close."

Just then, a scream broke the morning quiet. It seemed to come from a nearby house. Buck grabbed the sword that was slung across his back and jumped off his horse.

When the brother and sister reached the house, they heard the scream again. "It's coming from upstairs!" Agate said.

They raced up the wooden steps, pushed open a partly closed door, and stopped. A strange little girl was in a bed in the middle of the room. Her eyes were red and had tiny black pupils.

The girl tossed and screamed while a man and woman watched. The woman was sobbing. The man picked up a leather bag and said, "There's nothing more I can do here." He brushed past Agate and Buck and walked out of the door.

Agate held up her stone and watched as the glow faded. "This is it, Buck," she said quietly.

The woman turned to look at them. "Who are you?" she asked, trying to dry her tears.

"We were sent here to help," said Agate.

"I don't see what two children can do that Dr Copper couldn't," said the woman.

Agate and Buck looked at the girl, who was tossing and turning in her bed. She seemed more animal than human.

"What made her this way?" asked Buck.

The woman said, "Emily is possessed."

Agate said, "I'm not sure about that." She crouched down, found an old book in her satchel, and opened it. She turned the pages quickly, finally stopping when she found what she was looking for. "We need to examine her blood," she said.

Buck held Emily tight in his arms while Agate drew some blood from the girl's arm.

Then Agate noticed the mark on the back of the girl's neck.

"Have you ever seen a bite like this?" Agate asked Emily's mother.

"Never," said the mother. "And neither has Dr Copper. And he has been on trips to the Amazon. He's seen just about every type of insect bite there is."

After the blood was drawn, Agate set up the microscope she carried with her. Under the microscope's lens, Agate could see Emily's blood cells. They looked like tiny red bottle caps.

Agate adjusted the microscope. Then she saw something frightening. Mixed with Emily's blood cells were other, black cells. The black cells attached themselves to the red blood cells and punctured them. After just a few seconds, the black cells outnumbered the red ones.

"Whatever it is," said Agate, "it isn't friendly."

– Chapter 3 –

WHITE AS MOONLIGHT

Miles and miles away, in a seaside village on the coast of British Columbia, Wilson Fitch sat at the end of an old dock. He was doing some fishing in the cool summer evening.

The moon was out and a fog was beginning to move in. In the distance, Fitch saw a pair of red lights swooping across the sky. "What on earth?" he said, scrambling to his feet.

He watched as the lights circled in the sky and then headed straight towards him.

Fitch began running down the dock to shore. A buzzing sound grew louder and louder until it was all Fitch could hear.

When his boot caught on a loose board on the dock, he tripped. He rolled on to his back and saw the approaching red lights. And then he realized they weren't lights at all.

They were eyes!

Fitch screamed in terror.

Standing before him was a man, but it wasn't a normal man. This being had large insect wings, a mosquito head, clawed hands, and a long, sharp stinger for a mouth. Its eyes glowed red.

"Don't kill me!" yelled Fitch.

Just then, a small boat drifted up to the dock and a woman stepped out. She held a lantern. A cloak covered her long, straight hair, which was as white as moonlight.

Everything she wore was white, even her boots and gloves.

The monster did not hesitate. It picked up Fitch and took off into the night sky.

* * *

Back in Booker, Emily was sleeping peacefully on the barn floor. But her breathing sounded like a wild animal.

"I don't know what to do," said her mother. "It's almost as if she is changing into something else."

"We know some people that might be able to help," said Buck. "Right, Aggie?"

Agate sat on a stool leafing through one of her journals.

She didn't seem to hear them.

"Agate?" asked Buck. "Do you think we need to talk to the council?"

Agate's tongue stuck out of the corner of her mouth as she leafed through the book.

"I was thinking about that bite on her neck," said Agate. "It reminded me of something I saw in this book."

She pointed to a sketch in the book. It was a drawing of a human shoulder. The shoulder had a large insect bite on it. Three strange dots were in the middle of the bite.

"Emily has the same bite," said her mother. "What is it from?"

"The vampire mosquito," said Buck.

Agate smiled at Buck and said, "You've been reading Dad's journals, too."

Frowning, the woman looked at them. "What are you talking about?" she asked suspiciously. "A vampire mosquito?"

Agate began, "It's an old story."

She paused, collecting her thoughts before she started the tale. "The Tlingit people, who are native to these mountains, tell a story of a vampire giant. For centuries, the giant hunted and killed the Tlingit people. One year, the Tlingit leader sent his strongest warrior to defeat the giant."

Buck continued, "The warrior entered the giant's home. The giant was gone, but his son was there. The warrior asked how the giant could be killed and the son told him that the giant's heart was in his ankle."

Agate said, "So the warrior hid and waited for the vampire giant to return. When the giant walked past, the warrior stabbed the giant in the ankle. The monster fell. But as he died, he said, 'I will come back to drink the blood of your people until the end of time.'"

"What did the warrior do?" asked the mother.

"The warrior burned the giant's body so that he couldn't come back," said Buck. "Then he took the ashes and threw them into the wind. That was his big mistake."

"The ashes scattered," said Agate. "Each piece of ash turned into a mosquito."

"That is why mosquitoes drink blood," said Buck, "according to the Tlingit."

The mother stared down at the strange drawing in Agate's book. "That's just a fairy tale – a story," she said.

"Some stories are real," said Agate.

"Even if the story is real, you just said the mosquito king was dead," said Emily's mother. "So how could he make that mark on Emily's neck?"

"The giant was killed," said Buck. "But his son wasn't, and his son had children."

Chapter 4

COUNCIL OF ELDERS

That afternoon, Agate and Buck left Booker and headed west. They could see the mountains in the blue distance. Buck looked up at one of the nearby foothills. "Do you know where we are?" he asked.

Agate looked around at the trees. "Yes," she said. "We're close to Cutface Peak."

Buck smiled. Then his face grew sad. "Do you ever think about what happened there last autumn?"

"Of course I do," Agate said.

"I think about it all the time," said Buck.

Agate and Buck McGregor were not normal children. Their parents had been spirit hunters, warriors against the forces of evil. They were members of a tribe called the Majictaw, who had vowed to protect the world from danger and destruction.

The powerful Majictaw blood flowed through Agate and Buck's veins. The brother and sister had recently discovered a few of the powers they were born with. They had more powers, too, which they didn't yet know about.

Like their parents, Agate and Buck had sworn to protect the world from evil.

"I think about how Mum and Dad gave their lives to save us on Cutface Peak," Buck continued. "But I couldn't save them, and I let them down."

"You didn't let them down. You did everything you could," Agate said.

Buck shook his head. He said, "What if I am not strong enough? What if I won't be able to help defeat this mosquito thing?"

Agate looked at the sword that hung across Buck's back. "You have the Halynn'Pano."

The Halynn'Pano was a legendary sword. The spirit of every warrior who had used it had been absorbed into its powerful blade. Buck had inherited the ancient weapon.

"You're a warrior, Buck," Agate said. "Just like Dad and Mum. You just need to have faith in yourself."

"I hope you're right," Buck said.

"When am I wrong?" Agate said, smiling.

They kept riding. By nightfall, they found themselves in front of a steep cliff face.

This was the entrance to a temple where the Majictaw gathered. Inside were Agate and Buck's friends, the only people who would know what to do about the Mosquito King.

* * *

Agate and Buck stood in the middle of the temple's council room.

Large torches lit the room, casting shadows on the paintings that hung from the walls. The paintings were decorated with pictures of the sun, prairies, desert, seas, mountains, and forests.

The Council of Elders sat in the centre of the room. Igam, the oldest and most powerful Majictaw, sat in the middle. Four metal bowls were on his left and right. The bowls were filled with burning coals, each producing a different colour of fire. In the fire, the faces of the other elders appeared.

"We should do what is right," said one face. "The children should go to the village by the sea and seek out this Mosquito King."

"No," said Igam, holding up his hand. "They are too young and inexperienced. Mastiff will go. He is already preparing."

The elders grumbled and argued, but eventually they agreed. When everything was settled, the fires slowly died and the faces disappeared. The council meeting was over.

Agate and Buck left Igam alone in the council room. "What was that all about?" asked Agate. "Why doesn't Igam think we should go?"

Buck grabbed her shoulder. "If the council feels we aren't ready, then we aren't ready."

Agate shook off his hand "Of course we're ready. You know we can help defeat this monster."

"Aggie," Buck said, "we have to listen to the council. We may have been lucky before, but we have to do what they say. "

Agate shook her head at Buck. "You sound like you don't want to fight. What is wrong with you?"

Igam walked down the stone steps from the council room and stepped between Agate and Buck. "Calm your minds, children. I want you both to talk to Mastiff. You need to tell him what you saw."

– Chapter 5 –

WARRIORS

Down in the temple stables, Mastiff was gathering other Majictaw warriors.

Mastiff was an enormous man. He had long blond hair and a long blonde beard that fell in two braids. His eyes were as blue as arctic ice. He wore brown leather armour that was decorated with ancient wolf symbols.

When Agate and Buck arrived at the stables, Mastiff scooped Agate up into his strong arms and held her above his head.

"Aggie, my darling," he said. "What brings you into the stables? We haven't seen you in six months."

"Igam sent us here to tell you about the creature you may be fighting," she said.

"What creature is that?" Mastiff asked.

"A vampire giant," said Buck.

Mastiff beat his chest with his fist and said, "Good. I like a challenge."

Agate shook her head and said, "It's not him we're worried about. He's dead. But someone out there is doing his work. It looks like they're using mosquitoes as a weapon."

Sabina, another warrior, stepped forward. "What kind of weapon?" she asked.

"The mosquitoes carry a disease that attacks the victims' bloodstream," said Agate. "It looks like a mutative disease."

"In English, my dear girl," said Mastiff.

"Mutative means 'changing,'" Buck said. "The mosquitoes are changing people into vampires."

Mastiff laughed loudly and said, "Well, why didn't you say so?"

"You don't understand," said Agate. "I think he is creating an army."

Sabina pushed her long, red hair out of her face and asked, "Why does he need an army?"

"Revenge," said Buck.

"Well, it's a good thing I'm bringing the best," said Mastiff. "Sabina is good with a bow. And Lomas specializes in potions."

"Don't forget about me," said a woman's voice.

Agate and Buck turned around to see their old friend Calandra step into the stables.

"How could you two have grown so much in six short months?" she said, laughing.

"You have to let us go with you," Agate said.

"Did Igam say that?" asked Calandra.

"I don't care what he says," said Agate. "We're going with you!"

"Calm down, Aggie," said Buck.

Mastiff squatted down to Agate. "Don't worry, fireball. Your time will come."

Agate and Buck stayed long enough to watch the group ride off.

"They're making a mistake," said Agate. "We're the ones who found that little girl infected by the mosquito. It means we're supposed to put an end to this evil."

But as Buck watched the warriors leave, he couldn't help but feel relieved.

He felt Igam's decision was for the best. He and Agate were still too young for all this.

The children walked slowly up to the main chambers of the temple. After their parents had died, Agate and Buck had been taken in by the tribe and given their own rooms, high in a rocky tower.

Alone in his room, Buck gazed out the window at the starry night. He reached for his sword.

Moonlight from the window gleamed on the blade, revealing a line of magic symbols. Buck had memorized what the symbols said.

Draw your strength from their past.

In the shine of the blade, Buck saw the faces of past warriors.

Each warrior had been killed in battle using the sword.

Their faces seemed to swim deep within the glowing metal.

"Is Agate right?" Buck whispered to the blade. "Am I afraid of fighting? Should I have gone with Mastiff and the others?"

The blade was silent. Buck heard only the sound of the wind sighing through the pine trees far below his tower window.

– Chapter 6 –

AGATE'S FLIGHT

Buck wasn't able to sleep that night. He kept staring into the Halynn'Pano, looking for answers. Outside, the sun was gently rising, and Buck's room slowly filled with golden morning light.

Buck heard his stomach growl. He hadn't had dinner before going to his room, and now he was really hungry. And he was worried. Maybe he and Agate shouldn't have run away from that Mountie. Maybe they should have gone to their aunt and uncle's house after all.

Buck put down his sword and walked out of the room.

He knocked on Agate's door. "Aggie, I'm starving. I forgot to have dinner last night. Do you have anything to eat?"

Agate didn't answer.

Buck quietly opened her door. Agate was huddled beneath her blanket, sound asleep. Buck looked all around her room but did not find any food.

He bent down to tap Agate's shoulder, but before he could, he saw a loaf of bread where Agate's head should have been. Was he dreaming?

He pulled the blanket off of Agate's bed.

She was gone!

"Agate," said Buck to the empty room, "what have you done?"

* * *

Soon after she and Buck went to their rooms the night before, Agate had made a decision. She would follow Mastiff and the others into the battle.

She waited until she heard Buck's door close. Then she started arranging loaves of bread on her sleeping mat in the shape of a body. When she was satisfied with the shape, she snuck down to the stables and prepared her horse, Sunbeam, for the trip.

Once Sunbeam was saddled and ready, Agate patted the horse's neck and held the Pedne Stone in her other hand. Her father had given her that stone on the same day he chose her name: Agate, because she had as many layers as one of those smooth river stones.

"The Majictaw need me," Agate said softly to the stone.

She put the stone away, mounted Sunbeam, and quickly and quietly rode out of the stables.

Agate rode through the night and on into morning, stopping once to give Sunbeam a brief rest and some food and water. Agate thought she'd catch up to Mastiff and the others by nightfall.

* * *

"That was very unwise of her," said Igam. Buck had just finished telling him about Agate leaving.

"She thinks she can do anything," said Buck.

Igam laughed gently. "Well, you must prepare for your journey. She will need your help." The old man guided Buck down a long, dark corridor. At the end of the corridor, Igam pushed open a huge wooden door.

Behind the door was a steamy room with a large cauldron in its middle. The contents of the large pot, which sat over a coal fire, boiled and popped and hissed.

"We'll find what we need here," said Igam.

"If I want to catch up with Agate, shouldn't I be getting ready?" asked Buck. "She already has a head start. I'll never catch her if I don't leave right away."

Igam rummaged through some small bottles on a nearby table. He held up a small bottle made of dark blue glass. "Here it is," he said. The bottle was marked with an image shaped like a lightning bolt. Igam removed the cork from the bottle, and then took a sugar cube from a small tin container.

"What is that?" asked Buck.

"It's called Whi'Che Hadda," said Igam. "It means 'lightning in a bottle.'"

Igam was very careful as he tipped the bottle over the sugar cube. He allowed only one drop to spill from the bottle onto the sugar cube. The cube quickly absorbed the blue liquid until there was just a tiny blue dot on one side of the cube.

"More than one drop could be deadly," said Igam. He held the cube out to Buck.

Buck looked at it. "What does it do?"

Igam corked up the bottle and placed it back on the table. "Give this to Moonshine," said the old man, "but hold the reins tightly, or he may run out from under you. Now, go!"

Buck quickly ran to the stables and prepared his horse for the journey. He jumped onto Moonshine's back. Then he grabbed the reins in one hand and wrapped them around his wrist. He leaned down and held the sugar cube next to Moonshine's mouth.

The horse sniffed it and then ate it.

Moonshine immediately whinnied loudly and took off running.

Buck held on tight. Moonshine was running so fast that it seemed his hooves never touched the ground.

The wind tore at Buck's face, making it hard for him to breathe.

He watched the forest around him rush past him as a green blur. The sun overhead was just an orange stripe across the blue sky.

Now Buck understood why Igam had been careful to let only one drop of liquid fall onto the sugar cube. Any more and Moonshine would be running so fast that Buck would've fallen for sure.

Buck hoped that Moonshine would be able to stop once they reached Agate and the Majictaw warriors.

– Chapter 7 –

A GRAND ARMY

Miles away, at the base of the Rocky Mountains in British Columbia, was a town called Archer Pass.

High above the town, carved into one of the mountains, was a strange rock formation. The townspeople called it the castle, but legend said that it had once been the home of an evil bloodsucking giant.

Grown-ups laughed at this, but children shivered when they looked at the castle's dark shape.

Even some of the grown ups secretly believed the legend. Soon, they all would.

At the same time that Buck was riding towards his sister, a man was walking down the main street of Archer Pass, carrying a sack of flour on his shoulder. Suddenly, out on the horizon, a faded black cloud grew in the sky. The bearded man thought nothing of it until he heard the sound, a slight humming noise.

He stopped and watched as the cloud grew larger and blacker. The buzzing grew louder.

Other townspeople, hearing the strange sound, stepped out of their shops and homes to see what was going on.

As the black cloud grew closer, the man dropped his sack of flour and ran in the opposite direction.

Soon, the black cloud was directly over the town.

In one terrifying moment, the cloud burst into thousands of mosquitoes dropping out of the sky. The townspeople had never seen mosquitoes like them before. The flying creatures were the size of apples.

The town erupted in panic. People screamed and waved their arms around as they ran, trampling anyone in their way.

The insects bit people on their necks and faces and arms. Some people ran through town with insects stuck to them. Other people armed themselves with brooms. One man even pulled out a gun and started shooting into the sky.

The attack lasted an hour before stopping as quickly as it had started. Then Archer Pass was a ghost town. People lay on the ground, each one covered with bites from the vampire insects. Some people moaned. Others wept. A few still screamed.

Only one person did not get bitten –
Thomas Malloy.

When the Mountie had discovered that
Agate and Buck had deserted him, he went
after them. Their trail led him past Cutface
Peak. Then Malloy followed them to a steep
cliff side. Their horses' hoofprints seemed to
lead directly into the side of the mountain.
Malloy knew it had to be a trick, so he
kept searching.

After several days, his search led him to
Archer Pass.

Malloy planned to ask the townspeople
if they had seen any signs of a boy and girl
travelling together.

He was on the edge of the town, putting
his horse into a stable, when the attack came.
Malloy heard the strange buzzing and ran to
the stable door.

When he realized what was happening, he closed and bolted the doors. Then he covered his horse in thick blankets. He searched the stable floor for an entrance to a cellar. After a few minutes, he found an entrance hidden under scattered straw.

Quickly, Malloy raced down the ladder and closed the heavy wooden door above him. The buzzing sounded like the wail of a cyclone.

After an hour, it stopped. Malloy crept back up the ladder.

He peered out of the narrow crack between the two stable doors. Then he saw them.

The Mosquito King and his companion, a woman dressed in white, were walking through town. The man was a huge hulk of muscle, over eight feet tall. He had thick, bushy eyebrows and sideburns. Sharp fangs hung over his bottom lip and his red eyes burned like coals.

"My little ones don't bite just to feed," the Mosquito King said to the woman. "Now each one of these humans is infected. Soon they will be part of my grand army."

The woman in white bent down towards a man lying on the ground. "How long before the marked ones are fully changed?"

"Three or four days," said the king. "The change is painful. Some will not survive. The others will have my thirst for blood. Each one will become my slave. Soon, my ancestors and I will have our revenge!"

Chapter 8

STORIES

Agate met up with Mastiff and the other Majictaw after two days of riding. Mastiff was angry. "We must obey the council's decisions," he told her. "To defy them is to disrespect them. You must know that."

She did. But at the same time, Agate could tell that the rest of the Majictaw felt more at ease with her around.

Lomas prepared a pot of stew for the first night Agate was with the Majictaw in the mountains. Everyone ate and told stories.

Calandra told the tale of a shadow monster from another world that would snatch children and animals and then disappear.

"You all have such wonderful stories," said Agate. "I wish I had some."

Mastiff wiped his beard with the back of his hand and said, "You do have a story, fireball."

Sabina nodded. "In time you shall take our place," she said to Agate, "and tell your stories to the young ones."

"Everyone has their time," said Lomas. "Just have a little patience."

That night as the rest of the warriors fell asleep in their blankets, Agate took a walk.

Could the Majictaw be right? she wondered.

Would people talk about her someday and tell her adventures around a campfire?

What about Buck's story? Agate wondered what her brother had thought when he saw that she was gone.

She looked down at her Pedne Stone, and held it tightly in her fist. It was warm. Whenever she held it she felt stronger and more relaxed.

She closed her eyes and felt a wave of peacefulness wash over her.

When Agate opened her eyes, she saw tiny blue flames flickering at the ends of her fingertips. She quickly waved her hands and the flames went away.

How odd! She felt no burning or pain.

She looked up at the dark, unfamiliar trees surrounding her. Where was she?

She walked down a path, but it led to a dead end.

Finally, she looked down at her necklace again. It was glowing brightly, brighter than ever before. The stone glowed whenever danger was near.

Agate realized she was not alone. Red eyes pierced the shadows. The girl spun around. Everywhere she turned she saw red eyes.

She was surrounded.

From somewhere in the darkness, a deep voice muttered, "Do not scream. Do not warn the others."

The eyes came closer. Agate could feel the shadows closing in on her. She could smell their hideous breath. Something reached out of the darkness and grabbed her.

Suddenly, a blue flash lit up the forest. The monsters were knocked down by the burst.

"Get her!" ordered the deep voice.

Agate did the only thing she could think of. She ran.

She didn't care where she was going, as long as it was away from those horrible red eyes that were chasing her.

The monsters' claws grasped at her feet. One of them grabbed her ankle and dragged her to the ground. When she rolled onto her back, Agate saw dozens of red eyes staring down at her.

All of a sudden, a horse leapt over her and into the group of monsters, knocking the creatures to the ground. The rider jumped off the horse and drew a large sword, which shone in the moonlight.

"Buck!" cried Agate.

The mosquito vampires circled Buck, and each one was met by his flashing blade. Agate watched as each monster fell.

In the end, only Buck remained. The vampires had fallen or fled.

Buck walked over and helped Agate up. "Don't talk to me, Aggie," he said. "I'm still angry with you."

"But we're together now," she said. "Nothing can stop us."

Buck leapt up on Moonshine and held out his hand to his sister. "I wouldn't be so sure of that," said Buck. "Now, hurry!"

As Agate reached up to take Buck's hand, something large and powerful swooped out of the night sky.

It picked Agate up and lifted her away.

"Aggie!" yelled Buck. For a brief moment, he could hear his sister shouting in the distance. Then her voice faded away to nothing.

– Chapter 9 –

POWER

Buck rode into the Majictaw camp, shouting, "Agate is gone! He took her!"

Lomas jumped up. "The Mosquito King?" he asked.

"Yes," said Buck. "I had to fight his friends."

"Take us to the fallen," said Sabina. "If we are to fight a war, we'll need to know what it is we're fighting."

The group packed up camp and followed Buck.

When they reached the clearing where Agate had been captured, they found vampire creatures lying on the ground. Their stiff wings glittered in the gloomy dawn.

Mastiff knelt down and examined the stinger of one of the vampires. "They don't need any weapons. Look at the size of these stingers. They look like huge knives."

"No weapons and no armour," added Mastiff. "You know what that means."

"They rely on their numbers," said Sabina.

"All these creatures to find one girl," said Calandra. "Just think how many will fight in a real battle."

"We have to find Agate," cried Buck.

Lomas reached into his pack and pulled out a large map. "Where do we go next?" he asked.

"Look here," said Sabina. She pointed to the map at a small town in the Rocky Mountains. "Archer Pass. That is where they have taken her."

"How do you know?" asked Buck.

"There is a legend about a vampire castle in that town," Sabina said. "It is the place for us to begin our search."

Mastiff looked at the map and rubbed his beard. "We can reach it by nightfall," he said. "But we'll have to ride hard and fast with little rest."

"Let's ride, then," said Sabina. She had already mounted her horse and was ready to go. "Let's go!"

* * *

Agate stumbled along a cold corridor in the mountain castle.

Her hands were locked in shackles and she was being led by the huge Mosquito King himself. She didn't dare look at him. She kept her eyes on the rocky floor in front of her.

In his deep, awful voice the king said, "I don't know what she wants with you."

She? thought Agate.

"You are only a little girl," the king continued.

The Mosquito King could not see in the darkness, but Agate was smiling. Only a little girl? He didn't realize how powerful she was.

A vast room appeared out of the shadows. A large stone throne stood in the middle of the furthest wall.

The woman dressed in white was sitting on the throne. "Ah," she said. "The girl I've seen in my dreams."

The Mosquito King led Agate in front of the woman.

"Who are you?" the girl asked.

The woman stared at Agate. Her eyes were dark pits. "My name is Anool," she said.

"What do you want from me?" asked Agate.

Anool smiled. "I want nothing from you. I have something to teach you."

Agate looked at her suspiciously. "I don't need you to teach me anything."

Then Anool stood up. "I disagree," she said. She took off one of her white gloves and reached out toward Agate.

She gently touched Agate's forehead.

Whoosh!

Anool was thrown backward to the floor.

"What is this?" demanded the Mosquito King.

"There is power in you," gasped the woman. Anool looked at Agate and saw that the girl was free of her shackles. The whole time she had been standing in the throne room, Agate had been picking the locks.

"You think you're tricky?" said Agate. She reached up and grabbed the Pedne Stone in her hand.

Instantly, the girl disappeared.

The Mosquito King roared with anger.

Chapter 10

A WARNING

Agate didn't let go of the Pedne Stone until she had run far away from the throne room.

The stone had helped her escape. But she couldn't believe what had happened when Anool touched her forehead.

Agate found a small side door that led outside the castle. The air was cold and the wind blew fiercely on the mountain. How would she find her way down from the castle? How would she ever find her way back to Buck?

Agate found shelter from the blowing cold under a huddle of pine trees. She snuggled down near the base of the trees.

Agate rested her forehead against her hands. When Anool had touched her, she had sent Agate a message.

But as Agate saw it again in her mind, she realized it wasn't a message at all. It was a memory.

Agate closed her eyes and could see a small boy playing in a stream. The boy held a long stick. He poked the stick around in the water, and pulled out a leather strap with a shiny wet ornament hanging from the end. The gold disc had symbols carved on it. Agate recognized them as the same symbols on the paintings in the Majictaw temple. The boy ran his finger over the largest symbol, which looked like a shining sun.

When the child placed the disk in his hand, something happened. His whole body froze. Then he began scratching his hand and arm violently. It looked as if something was entering his body through the gold disc. His eyes closed.

When the child's eyes opened again, something was different. His eyes no longer carried the innocence of a child. They were dark, and something evil lived in them.

The child turned and walked away. Then he started running. Before long, he had disappeared into the forest.

Agate blinked her eyes and wondered. She had seen that gold disc before. Her father was wearing it around his neck the last time she saw him, right before he stopped the evil creature called Coyote. Her father hadn't killed Coyote. He had trapped him in that gold disc.

The boy had absorbed Coyote's spirit. But where was this boy?

Agate closed her eyes to concentrate. Her mind was full of different images she could not understand. She saw the boy riding in the back of a wagon. Then he climbed over a mountain. Then he walked through a forest.

At last, the images slowed down and Agate saw the boy in an old temple. Vines covered the walls of the temple, and there was a hole in the ceiling.

The boy stood by an altar with two older men. Anool, the woman dressed in white, was chained to the altar. The boy stepped forward and grabbed her hand. Their hands glowed.

After a few moments, the boy let go. He ran out of the temple.

The two older men stepped towards the woman and unlocked her chains.

Anool sat up and looked at the men. Her eyes were deep pits filled with stars.

Almost instantly, the men shrivelled to skeletons and fell to the floor. Then Anool calmly walked out of the temple.

Agate shook her head. She couldn't believe what she was seeing. She was confused. Had Coyote left the boy's body and gone into the body of the woman in white? But the woman, or Coyote, had touched Agate on the forehead. Why would he give her those memories? Why would Coyote reveal himself to her?

Agate thought harder. Maybe Coyote hadn't completely taken over Anool's body. Perhaps the memories were Anool's way of warning Agate about Coyote.

Agate shivered as she huddled below the trees. "I have to find Buck," she said to herself. "I have to warn him."

Chapter 11

THE LEGENDS ARE TRUE

Buck, leading Agate's horse, finally arrived at Archer Pass with the other Majictaw warriors. The town was deserted. There were purses, umbrellas, hats, and even a set of false teeth scattered on the ground. They had been left by the townspeople during the attack.

"The people left in a hurry," said Calandra.

Buck looked up into the mountains. "It was the Mosquito King. He was here with his warriors."

"We shouldn't be so quick to assume," said Lomas. "Let's take a look for ourselves." He removed a pouch from his belt and poured a fine, red powder into his hand. With a blow of breath, the powder floated all around them. After a few seconds, images appeared in the air.

In the red dust clouds, the Majictaw saw the mosquito swarm grow, move in, and then attack the townspeople.

Lomas waved his hand and the wind blew the dust images away.

"As frightening as that was, that is still no army," said Lomas.

"Insects?" asked Mastiff. "We were sent here to stop some insects?"

Thomas Malloy walked out from behind a tree. "I think it's more than just bugs," he said.

"You!" Buck said. "Did you follow me?"

The Mountie ignored him. "Shortly after the attack," he said, "a strange man and woman arrived in town. The man was huge! And the woman was dressed all in white."

Buck asked, "What did they come to this town for?"

"That was the strange thing," said Malloy. "They looked like they were inspecting the damage the mosquitoes had done. And they said the people who were bitten would start to change. I'm not sure what that means."

"We don't have much time," Buck said. "His army may be ready. I need to find Agate."

"I saw her," said Malloy. He looked at Buck. "Last night. One of the creatures carried her toward the Mosquito King. Over there." Malloy pointed to the castle-shaped rock in the mountains.

"So the legends are true," said Sabina.

Mastiff said, "I may have been wrong back at the temple. If there is an army out there, we're going to need help."

Buck said, "You don't need me. You can handle this on your own."

Thomas Malloy stared at him. "So, you're planning on running off again, are you?"

Buck looked down at his feet, and then up at the Mountie. "I'm sorry we ran away from you," he said. "But we had to. People needed our help."

"Like your sister does now," said Malloy.

"I can take care of her myself," said Buck, quickly mounting his horse.

Then he rode away, heading in the direction of the Mosquito King's mountain castle.

– Chapter 12 –

REVENGE

In the highest tower of the castle, Anool stood and looked out of a window and across the mountains. Far off in the distance, the Pacific Ocean glistened in the light.

Carefully, Anool reached down to the brooch that held her white cloak. She unclasped it and let her cloak fall to the floor.

Then she changed out of her white clothes and into the bone armour that the mosquito guards wore.

When she was dressed, she took out a small piece of paper and wrote a letter. She wrapped the paper tightly around an arrow and tied it with string. She loaded the arrow into her crossbow and aimed it out of the window. When she pulled the trigger, the arrow shot across the castle and stuck in the ground by the gate.

Then she looked up and in to a cracked mirror on the wall. Anool saw that the image in the mirror was not her own. It was a man who looked like a rotting skeleton.

The creature pointed at Anool. "What are you doing?" he said. "You know you cannot overpower me. I am Coyote. I have lived for thousands of years."

Anool pointed back at the disgusting vision in the mirror and said, "You'll regret ever bringing me here."

With a thrust of Anool's hand, Coyote's reflection flew backwards in the mirror. He slowly stood up and started laughing.

He raised his hand and clutched the air as if he was choking Anool. Outside the mirror, Anool held her throat and gasped for breath as she collapsed to the floor.

When she stood back up, Coyote's reflection was in the mirror. Anool brushed herself off, and so did Coyote in the mirror.

"Now I am in control," Coyote said.

Then Coyote, in Anool's body, walked out of the room. She walked down the tower staircase and out on to a balcony.

There the Mosquito King sat on an old stone throne. He was in his human form. Coyote, in Anool's body, leaned over and whispered into the giant's ear. The king stood up and walked to the edge of the balcony.

A thousand vampire mosquito guards were in the castle below. The King drew his long white sword. He held it above his head and yelled, "The time has come for our revenge!"

The roar of buzzing wings filled the air. Like a giant, living cloud of darkness, the vampire army took flight and flew out into the mountains. The army headed toward Archer Pass.

As the sun loomed over the horizon, the black swarm filled the sky. The black cloud grew and grew until it was over the village of Archer Pass. Then the vampire mosquito guards dropped from the sky and began roaming the streets of the village.

A hundred vampires patrolled the main road through the village. A roaring wind rolled in from above. The wind brought clouds of red dust that formed into giant eagles and hawks.

The magical dust birds opened their beaks, plucked the vampires from the ground, and flew them away.

From his hiding spot inside the town's church tower, Lomas watched the vampires entering Archer Pass. His hand was full of red powder. As he carefully blew on it, the powder scattered out of the window and formed into giant eagle shapes.

Outside the village, Calandra watched from a perch high in a pine tree while more vampire guards roamed beneath the tall trees. Their wings and stingers twitched.

She smiled to herself, then tossed a handful of small seeds into the air.

Little seeds fell all around the mosquito guards. One of the guards picked one of the seeds up and examined it. It was a small green seed that looked like a pea.

The seed erupted into a monstrous thorny vine. The other seeds scattered around the guards quickly sprouted into large vines, too, wrapping the monsters in their thorny embrace.

Standing high in the pine tree, Calandra looked down at the trapped mosquito guards. She smiled again and tied her seed pouch tightly to her belt.

So far, so good, she thought to herself.

Chapter 13

THE SHAD'RI

Buck quickly rode his horse up the mountain. He stopped when he realized that large boulders had fallen across the pass ahead of him. He jumped off Moonshine, tied up his horse, and began climbing to the castle on foot. Behind him, the sun was setting into the ocean.

While riding, Buck had seen the dark buzzing cloud of vampire mosquitoes flying out of the mountain and heading toward Archer Pass.

He was sure his friends would be able to defeat the evil creatures, but he felt an icy cold in the pit of his stomach.

He hoped that Agate would be safe at the castle. As he neared the front gate, Buck saw a movement by the side of the path. He quickly drew the Halynn'Pano. But a familiar voice stopped him.

"Buck! It's me!"

"Agate?" cried Buck.

The girl ran to her brother and threw her arms around him. "Oh, Buck," she said. "It's Coyote! He's come back!"

"What do you mean?" asked the boy.

Agate explained what had happened to her. She told Buck about the strange woman who had touched her forehead, and who was filled with the evil spirit of Coyote.

"I think we can defeat Coyote this time," said Agate. "You know, Igam once told me that my Pedne Stone could make time stand still. But he was wrong. It doesn't freeze time. It makes me go faster. That's how I escaped when the Mosquito King got me."

"Just don't rely on it, Aggie," Buck said.

"What do you mean?" asked Agate.

Buck looked down. "I did the very same thing once," he said. "I thought having this sword would be a piece of cake. Then I lost the sword, and I almost died. I don't want you to make the same mistake as I did."

Agate looked at Buck and said, "All right. I won't use it unless I have to."

Buck looked relieved. "Okay," he said. "When we get into the castle, you take the Mosquito King, and I'll take Coyote." Behind them, the sun was sinking into the ocean.

"Whatever you say," said Agate. "But where are the Majictaw?"

Buck looked down the mountain. "They have problems of their own right now."

The two children approached the gate of the castle.

Agate noticed an arrow lying on the ground just past the gates. She picked it up. A piece of parchment had been rolled on to the arrow's shaft.

"Is that a note?" Buck asked.

Agate unrolled the parchment and began reading.

"Agate, I am writing to tell you that I have failed," Agate read aloud. "I cannot hold off Coyote any longer. His powers are far too strong. I have hidden my belongings in the high tower. Find them, and they are yours to keep. Use them to defend the others."

Agate looked up at Buck. "It must be from Anool," she said.

"Who is this woman?" Buck asked.

"I believe that she was a powerful Majictaw who died," said Agate. "You see, some Majictaw have the ability to be summoned from the beyond. They are called the Shad'Ri. Their spirits can be pulled back into physical bodies. It can only happen at special times and during sacred rituals. I read about it in one of Dad's journals. I think Anool must be one of the Shad'Ri."

"That's amazing," Buck said.

Agate took a deep breath. "I've heard it said that you and I may be Shad'Ri once we have carried out our mission here on earth."

Buck shuddered. "Let's not talk about that," he said. "What does Coyote want with the Shad'Ri woman?"

"When Coyote takes someone's body, he can harvest their spirit, making his own even more powerful," said Agate.

She paused and stared at her brother. "How strange," Agate said. "I didn't know about Coyote doing that until you just asked me."

Buck shook his head. "I don't know, Aggie. Ever since this Anool woman touched your forehead, you have been acting strange."

"I am not acting strange on purpose," said Agate. "Now can we get to that tower? I want to find my things."

"Your things?" Buck asked.

Agate shook her head. "Did I say my things? I meant Anool's things. You're right, I really am acting weird."

The two young Majictaw warriors walked up to the giant's castle and through the gates.

– Chapter 14 –

A BATTLE

The sun was nearly gone. Night was approaching. Agate pointed to a tall castle tower where she saw light in a window. "There's Anool's tower," she said.

Buck looked around and saw a small door. "We can get in over there," he said.

The inside of the tower was lit by torches. Shadows danced on the walls. Agate and Buck walked through several corridors before they found a spiral set of steps that led towards the top of the tower.

They climbed the steps and finally found Anool's room. The first thing they saw was the large cracked mirror.

"Something bad happened here," said Buck. "I can feel it."

They began searching the room for Anool's hidden things. After a few moments, Buck noticed a loose stone in the wall. He pulled it out and found a bag in the gap behind the wall. Then he reached inside the bag and took out a crossbow and cloak.

"Nice gear," Buck said. He found a coil of thin rope and said, "I wonder what she used this for."

Agate said, "Grappling, probably. She ties the rope to a kind of arrow and uses it to climb to high places."

Buck examined the rope more closely.

"What's that sound?" asked Agate.

Buck ignored her. He was staring at the rope. "This Anool must have been a fierce warrior," he said.

Suddenly, a dark shape swooped through the window, grabbed Buck, and flew away. Agate leaned out of the window and screamed.

Buck looked down at the tower and watched Agate's terrified face growing smaller and smaller. The Mosquito King, with Buck in his claws, flew higher into the sky.

Buck had to do something fast. He realized that he was still holding Anool's rope. He quickly tied one end into a lasso.

The Mosquito King turned his head towards Buck. "Coyote spoke highly of your father and of you," he said. "But I don't see what's so special about you. All I have to do is let go and you will smash on the rocks below, like an acorn!"

Just as the Mosquito King released Buck from his grip, Buck tossed his lasso over the King's head.

Buck fell like a stone, but the rope tightened and jerked the Mosquito King down with him. They fell onto a high bridge that connected the tower to the castle.

Buck's shoulder instantly stung badly from the fall. By the time he drew his sword, the Mosquito King had already shed the rope around his neck.

"You will pay for that, little human!" the king screamed.

The Mosquito King spread his wings, drew his sword, and charged.

With one quick dodge and two swings of his sword, Buck clipped the king's wings.

The monster shrieked in pain and turned around to face him.

The Halynn'Pano seemed to have a life of its own. Clash! Clang! Their swords echoed as Buck fought the Mosquito King.

Buck was strong, but the Mosquito King was bigger and stronger. They crossed swords over the edge of the bridge and the king loomed over Buck's face. The king had long fangs and dark, bushy eyebrows. He said, "You're going to lose. I'm too strong for you."

"You're stronger than me. But I have more than strength on my side," Buck said.

The Majictaw sword pulled Buck away from the edge of the bridge. The boy spun around, swift as a breath, causing the king to stumble forward. The giant's knees were higher than the stone edge of the bridge. His monstrous weight tipped him over the edge. Buck heard the king shriek as he fell.

– Chapter 15 –

STRANGE DREAM

Back in Archer Pass, the vampire mosquito army was still hunting for the other Majictaw warriors.

A group of mosquito guards roamed the outskirts of the town. Their feelers were twitching and they made odd clicks and whistles as they patrolled.

A large rock dropped from the sky and crushed all but two of the soldiers. The two remaining soldiers drew their swords.

"Looking for me?" asked Mastiff, appearing behind them.

The guards turned around and Mastiff instantly grabbed them both. His powerful hands cracked the wings of the insect creatures. Then his sword finished them off.

In a street in Archer Pass, Sabina knelt in deep meditation. All around her, the last of the vampire mosquito army approached. Everything was quiet and dark except for Sabina's armour, which glowed orange in the twilight. As the army slowly crept in on her, her armour glowed brighter.

When the insect soldiers drew their swords, a pattern showed up on Sabina's armour, glowing brightly. The vampires watched as an image shaped like a large bird spread its wings across Sabina's armour. The armour shone as bright as the sun, forcing the vampire mosquitoes to cover their eyes.

Then a flash of energy burst from Sabina's armour. The soldiers were turned into a pile of smoking ash.

Mastiff, Lomas, and Calandra found Sabina in the village. Smoke rose from Sabina as she stood up and took off her armour.

"That never ceases to amaze me," Mastiff told Sabina, who wiped sweat from her face and smiled.

The four Majictaw heard a buzzing noise.

"What's that noise?" Calandra asked.

"Buzzing!" said Lomas. "More soldiers?"

"No," said Sabina. "Look!" She pointed towards the centre of the town.

The buzzing sound was voices – human voices.

The townspeople of Archer Pass were wandering through the streets.

They looked tired and confused, as if they had just woken up from a strange dream.

"The power of the Mosquito King is broken!" yelled Mastiff.

Sabina looked up at the rocky castle in the mountains. "Is it?" she said. "I wonder."

* * *

In the castle tower, Agate strapped Anool's crossbow to her back and ran down the spiral steps. She had to help Buck!

As she reached the main hallway, the torches on the wall went out one by one. Darkness surrounded her. Agate felt her way along the damp, stone wall. She headed toward the only light she could see.

When she reached the light, Agate realized she was in the throne room. And Coyote, in Anool's body, was sitting on the throne.

"Anool thought highly of you," said Coyote. "I guess she grew fond of you in that brief encounter you and she had."

Agate drew her short bronze sword. "We've stopped you," she said. "Your army of vampires is defeated. You are defeated."

Coyote stood and said, "Am I?"

Agate reached up to her necklace and grabbed the Pedne Stone. All around her, time seemed to stop. Even Coyote froze. Agate ran across the floor and stood behind Coyote, ready to sink her sword into the demon's skin.

As soon as she got close to Coyote, time seemed to return to its normal speed. Coyote swung around and grabbed Agate by the throat. He threw her across the room. But Agate didn't smash into the wall. Instead, Coyote held the girl in midair with Anool's powers.

Unable to move, Agate faced her enemy. She felt alone. All Agate could do was look at the monster in Anool's body.

A blade flew out of the darkness and sliced off Coyote's hand. The monster screamed. Agate fell from Coyote's grip and landed hard on the stone floor.

When she looked up, she saw Buck and Coyote crossing swords as they rushed into the dark hallway.

Agate heard their swords clanging up the spiral stairs to the tower. She followed the noises and rushed up the stone steps that led to Anool's old room. She entered the room as Coyote swung hard and knocked Buck's sword from his hand.

"Enough of this playing around," said Coyote, raising a handless arm. "It is time to dispose of you, once and for all. Prepare to meet your parents!"

A stone block hovered above Buck's head. It was the stone he had pulled out from the wall when he found Anool's hidden bag.

Coyote's head cocked in curiosity. Suddenly, Coyote's body was hit by the stone, sending the evil being out of the window and into the rocky shadows below the castle.

Buck stood up. He turned to look at his sister. Agate's crossbow was armed and aimed right at his heart.

It is Anool, thought Buck. Anool's spirit was inside Agate's body.

Anool had touched the girl's forehead. Now Agate had been taken over by Coyote.

Buck waved his arms and said, "Agate, stop! You don't want to hurt me."

It was too late. Agate pulled the trigger of the crossbow and the arrow whizzed towards Buck.

Time seemed to slow down. Buck couldn't believe his sister had shot at him. He opened his mouth to scream, and then the arrow flew past and stuck into something behind him.

Buck turned around. The Mosquito King was standing right behind him. And the arrow that Agate had shot was sticking out of the king's ankle.

The monster gurgled once and fell to the floor, dead.

"His heart is in his ankle," said Agate. "Remember the story?"

Buck wrapped his arms around Agate. "You read too many books," he said, smiling.

"Lucky for you," Agate replied. She smiled. "Maybe one day there will be one about us."

LEGEND OF THE MOSQUITO

The character of the monstrous Mosquito King is based on a real Native American legend.

Long ago, the legend says, a giant appeared. He began destroying villages. The giant captured villagers and killed them, and then drank their blood. This went on for a long time, until one brave warrior came up with a clever plan to defeat the giant.

The warrior lay down in a place where the giant would find him. Then he pretended to be dead. The giant scooped him up and carried him back to his den.

Once he was in the giant's home, the warrior jumped up, surprising the giant, and struck him down.

"You will never defeat me," said the giant as he died. "I will take my revenge against all humans."

To make sure that the giant's evil promise would never come true, the warrior cut the giant's body into hundreds of pieces. Then he burned the pieces in a fire.

The warrior scattered the giant's ashes in the wind. He thought he was safe. But then something terrible happened. The tiny specks of ash turned into bloodthirsty mosquitoes.

To this day, according to the legend, mosquitoes continue to attack humans. They seek blood in revenge for the death of their master, the giant Mosquito King.

ABOUT THE AUTHOR

Scott R. Welvaert lives with his wife and two daughters. He has written many children's books. Most recently, he has written about Helen Keller and Thomas Edison. Scott enjoys reading and writing poetry and stories. He also enjoys playing computer games and watching the Star Wars films with his children.

ABOUT THE ILLUSTRATOR

Brann Garvey studied art and visual communications and has a degree in illustration. Brann is usually found with one or more of the following: a pencil in his hand, a comic book, a remote for watching DVDs, or his pet cat, Iggy. When the weather is nice, Brann likes to play frisbee golf. Iggy does not play.

GLOSSARY

elder someone who is older. In some societies, elders are respected and wise.

Halynn'Pano Buck's magical sword

microscope instrument that makes very small things look bigger

Mountie member of the Royal Canadian Mounted Police. The police ride on horses.

mutative something that causes something else to change

revenge action that someone takes to pay someone else back for harm done

satchel bag or small suitcase, sometimes carried over the shoulder

Shad'Ri Majictaw warrior who has died, but can be brought back to the living world during a special time and ritual

warrior soldier, or someone who fights battles

DISCUSSION QUESTIONS

1. Throughout this story, Buck tells Agate to be patient and not rush into things. Have you ever rushed in to something? What happened? What could you have done differently?

2. At the beginning of the book, Agate and Buck are heading to their aunt and uncle's house. What do you think might have happened if they had gone there as planned? Talk about the different things that could have happened.

3. Buck and Agate take a lot of risks in this book. Talk about the risks they take. Did they make good decisions or bad ones? Explain your thoughts.

WRITING PROMPTS

1. This book is based on a myth that explains why mosquitoes exist. Pick another animal or insect and write your own story about how they came to exist.

2. In this book, the town of Archer Pass is attacked by a horde of mosquitoes. Pretend you are a newspaper reporter, and write a story for the *Archer Pass News* about the event.

3. Agate and Buck have a number of adult friends who protect them and also respect them. Do you have any adults in your life like that? Describe them. If you don't have a close adult friend, describe what you would look for in an adult friend.

OTHER BOOKS IN THE SERIES